nickelodeon

SHIMMER and Shine™

Magical Pet Friends!

A Random House PICTUREBACK® Book

Random House 🏠 New York

© 2018 Viacom International Inc. All rights reserved. Published in the United States by Random House Children's Books, a division of Penguin Random House LLC, 1745 Broadway, New York, NY 10019, and in Canada by Penguin Random House Canada Limited, Toronto. Pictureback, Random House, and the Random House colophon are registered trademarks of Penguin Random House LLC. Nickelodeon, Nick Jr., Shimmer and Shine, and all related titles, logos, and characters are trademarks of Viacom International Inc.
rhcbooks.com
ISBN 978-0-525-58014-0
Printed in the United States of America
10 9 8 7 6 5 4 3 2 1

When it comes to having a great time, Tala and Nahal make every day *pet*-tacular for Shimmer and Shine!

Nahal is Shine's furry Bengal tiger cub. She is silly and feisty, and can be a bit of a scaredy-cat when it comes to loud noises. But she's still the *purr*-fect genie companion!

Tala is Shimmer's pet monkey. She loves shiny things and playing dress-up. She's an excellent climber, and her secret talent is juggling pineapples!

Tala's favorite game is hide-and-seek!

Nahal is an expert in one of her favorite activities—napping!

Not only do Tala and Nahal love Shimmer and Shine—
they love each other, too!

When Shimmer and Shine hop on their magic carpet, Tala and Nahal go with them!

On bright, sunny days, the genies and their pets love visiting Bela Beach.

Tala plays with a shell, and Nahal digs in the sand.

In the market, they greet their friend, Leah. They say hello to Leah's pet, a pretty purple fox named Parisa.

Parisa is smart and playful, and she can make her tail get really, really fluffy! She happily joins in Nahal and Tala's mischief-making fun.

Parisa has a very special talent. She can change the color of her fur to blend into her surroundings!

There are other wonderful pets in Zahramay Falls, too. Princess Samira's pet is an elegant peacock named Roya. Roya has beautiful tail feathers and loves to attend fancy masquerade balls.

Once a year, Roya loses a single feather. It can be used to magically repair a broken object!

Nazboo is Zeta's loyal pet dragon. Whenever the sneaky sorceress is riding on her flying scooter, Nazboo is right next to her.

Though he does his best to help Zeta on her missions, Nazboo is usually focused on finding his next snack!

Zain is a Ziffilon, a huge bird with a blue body and golden wings. He is the pet of Zac's genie, Kaz. Kaz befriended the feathered giant by feeding him Zlam berries.

Zain is the largest pet in Zahramay Falls. He can carry Kaz and others on his back!

Whether furry, feathered, or scaled, the pets of Zahramay Falls are always ready for awesome adventures!